Origami Math

Grades 4–6

BY **KAREN BAICKER**

New York • Toronto • London • Auckland • Sydney
Mexico City • New Delhi • Hong Kong • Buenos Aires

Teaching *Resources*

For my sister Kate Baicker.

Thanks to my editor Sarah Longhi
for the paper folding sessions, geometry
lessons, and patience; and to Maria Lilja
for the excellent design.

"Handy Envelope" activity on pages 11-13 is adapted from *Easy Origami: Amazing Activities for Hands-On Learning Across the Curriculum* by Gay Merrill Gross and Tina Weintraub. Copyright © 1995 by Gay Merrill Gross and Tina Weintraub. Reprinted by permission of the authors and Scholastic Inc.

Cover and interior design by Maria Lilja

Interior illustrations by Jason Robinson

Contents

Introduction

Why fold? The learning behind the fun

The first and most obvious benefit of teaching with origami is that it's fun and motivating for students. But the opportunities for learning through paper folding go much further. Many mathematical principles "unfold" and basic measurement and computation skills are reinforced as each model takes shape. The activities in this book are all correlated with NCTM (National Council of Teachers of Mathematics) standards, which are highlighted in each lesson.

In addition, origami teaches the value of working precisely and following directions. Students will experience this with immediacy when a figure does not line up properly or does not match the diagram. Also, because math skills are integrated with paper folding, a physical activity, students absorb the learning on a deeper level. Origami helps develop fine motor skills, which in turn enhances other areas of cognitive development.

Best of all, origami offers a sense of discovery and possibility. Make a fold, flip it over, open it up—and you have created a new shape or structure!

Tactile Learning Suppose you want to see if two shapes are the same size. You can measure the sides to get the information you need about area. But the easiest way to see if two objects are the same size is to place one on top of the other. That's essentially what you are doing when you fold a piece of paper in half. Similarly, you can bisect angles with a protractor, and you can calculate the third leg of a triangle—but never with such intuitive understanding as when you crease that angle and line up the sides with a simple origami fold.

Spatial Reasoning Origami activities challenge students to look at a diagram and anticipate what it will look like when folded. Often, two diagrams are shown and the reader must imagine the fold that was necessary to take the first image and produce the second. These are complex spatial relations problems—but ever so rewarding when the end result is a photo frame or a swan!

Symmetry With origami, when you make a fold in half, you create congruent shapes on either side of the fold, which clearly marks the line of symmetry.

Fractions Folding a piece of paper is a very concrete way to demonstrate fractions. Fold a piece of paper in half to show halves, and in half again to show quarters. For younger students, you can shade in sections to show parts and a whole. For older students, you can explore fractions. You can even show fraction equivalencies. Is $\frac{2}{3}$ of $\frac{1}{2}$ the same as $\frac{1}{2}$ of $\frac{2}{3}$? Through paper folding, you can see that it is!

Sequence With origami, it is critical to follow directions in a precise sequence. The consequences of skipping a step are immediate and obvious.

Geometry Most of the basic principles of geometry—point, line, plane, shape—can be illustrated through paper folding. One example is Euclid's first principle, that there is one straight line that connects any two points. This postulate becomes obvious when you make a fold that connects two points on the paper. For another example, older students are told that the angles of a triangle add up to 180°. Folding a triangle can prove this geometric fact, as you see in the diagrams below. You can also demonstrate the concepts of hypothesis and proof. Predict what will happen, and then fold the paper to test the hypothesis.

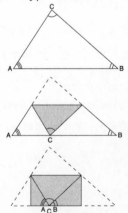

How to Use This Book

The lessons in this book are organized from very simple to challenging; all are geared toward the interests, abilities, and math skills of fourth, fifth, and sixth graders. Both the math concepts and the origami models are layered to reinforce and build on earlier lessons. Nonetheless, the lessons also stand independently and you may select them according to the interests and needs of your class, in any order.

In each lesson, you will find a list of Math Concepts, Math Vocabulary, and NCTM Standards that highlight the math skills addressed. At the heart of each lesson is Math Wise!, a script of teaching points and questions designed to help you incorporate math concepts with every step on the student activity page. Look for related activities to help students further explore these concepts at the end of the lesson in Beyond the Folds!

Step-by-step illustrations showing exactly how to do each step in the origami activity appear on a reproducible activity page following the lesson. Encourage students to keep these diagrams and bring them home so that the skills and sequence can be reinforced through practice. A reproducible pattern for creating the activity is also included for each lesson. The pattern is provided for your convenience, though you may use your own paper to create the activities. The pattern pages feature decorative designs that enhance the final product and provide students with visual support, including folding guide lines and ★s that help them position the paper correctly. To further support students' work with origami and math, you may also want to distribute copies of reference pages 7 and 8, The Language and Symbols of Origami and Basic Geometric Shapes Reference Sheet.

Origami on the Web

There are many great websites for teaching origami to children. Here are some recommended resources:

www.origami.com This comprehensive site also sells an instructional video for origami in the classroom.

www.origami.net This site is a good clearinghouse for information and resources related to origami.

www.paperfolding.com/math This excellent site explores the mathematics behind paper folding. Although geared for older students, it provides a useful overview for teachers.

www.mathsyear2000.org Click on "Explorer" to find some math-related origami projects with step-by-step illustrations, suitable for elementary students.

Tips for Teaching with Origami

Prepare for the lesson

- Try the activity ahead of time if possible. Moving through the steps helps you anticipate any areas of difficulty students may encounter and your completed activity provides a model for them to consult.

- Review the Math Wise! section and think through the mathematical concepts you want to highlight. You can find helpful definitions for the lesson's vocabulary list in the glossary on page 47.

- Photocopy the step-by-step instructions found in the lesson and the activity patterns (or have other paper ready for students to use).

Teach the lesson

- Familiarize students with the basic folding symbols on page 7.

- Introduce or review the origami terminology students will use in the lesson. Note that communication is enhanced when you can describe a specific edge, corner, or fold with precision.

- When possible, use the language of math as well as the language of origami when creating these projects. By saying, "Here I am dividing the square with a valley fold," you reinforce geometry concepts as well as the folding sequence. Some of the ideas expressed in the Math Wise! notes in the lesson plan may sound sophisticated. Yet, by using

the proper language as you make the folds, you will begin to teach students concepts that become the foundation for success with math in later grades. You'll be surprised at how much they grasp in the context of creating the origami.

- Demonstrate the folds with a larger piece of paper. Make sure the paper faces the way the students' paper is facing them.

- Support students who need more help with following directions or with manipulating spatial relationships by marking landmarks on the paper with a pencil as you go around the classroom. You can make a dot at the point where two corners should meet, for example.

- Arrange the class in clusters, and let students who have completed one fold assist other students. This will foster cooperative learning, and help you address all students' questions.

Fold accurately

- Make sure students fold on a smooth, hard, clean surface.

- Encourage students to make a soft fold and check that the edges line up properly to avoid overlapping. They can also refer to the diagram and make sure that the folded shape looks correct. After they make adjustments, they can make a sharper crease using their fingernail.

Choose your paper

- You can reproduce the patterns in this book onto copy paper. However, you can also use packs of origami paper, or cut your own squares. Keep in mind that thinner paper is easier to fold. Gift wrap, catalogues, magazines, menus, calendars, and other scrap paper can make wonderful paper for these projects. It is best to work with paper where the two sides, front and back, are easily distinguished.

Encourage students to explore geometry

- Unfold a shape just to look at the interesting pattern you have created through your series of creases. Challenge students to create their own variations—and make their own diagrams showing how they did it.

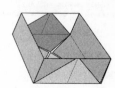

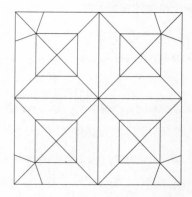

Box unfolded

The Language and Symbols of Origami

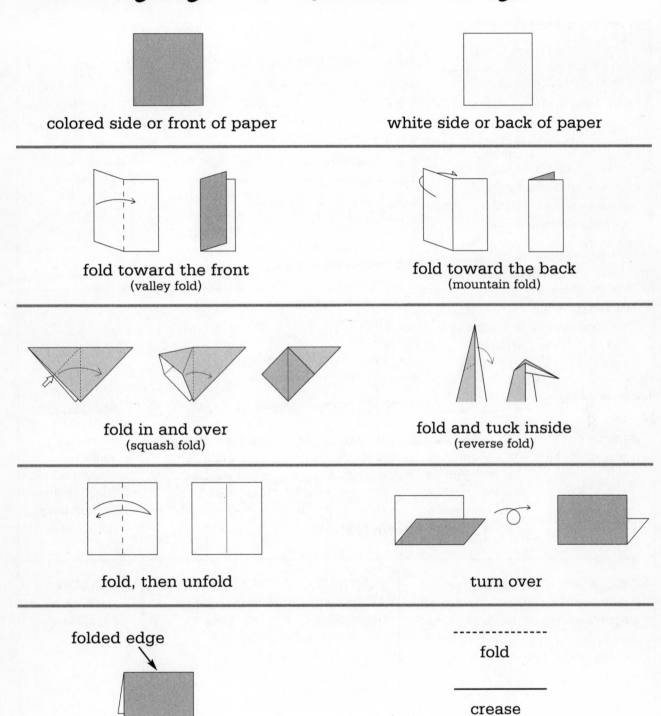

colored side or front of paper

white side or back of paper

fold toward the front
(valley fold)

fold toward the back
(mountain fold)

fold in and over
(squash fold)

fold and tuck inside
(reverse fold)

fold, then unfold

turn over

folded edge

raw edge

------------- fold

_____ crease

✂ -·-·-·-·- cut

Basic Geometric Shapes Reference Sheet

CONGRUENT
equal in measurement

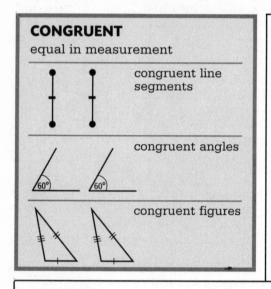

congruent line segments

congruent angles

congruent figures

QUADRILATERALS
A **quadrilateral** is any figure that has four sides.

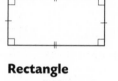

Parallelogram
a quadrilateral that has two pairs of parallel sides and two pairs of congruent sides

Rectangle
a quadrilateral that has four right angles (90°). All rectangles are parallelograms

Square
a quadrilateral that has four right angles and four congruent sides. All squares are rectangles

TRIANGLES
A **triangle** is any figure that has three sides.

 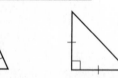 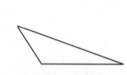

Right triangle
a triangle with a right angle

Isosceles triangle
a triangle with two congruent sides and two angles equal in measurement

Isosceles right triangle
a triangle with two congruent sides, and one right angle

Scalene triangle
a triangle with no congruent sides and no congruent angles

Equilateral triangle
a triangle with three congruent sides and three congruent angles

CIRCLE
a round shape measuring 360°

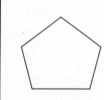

OVAL
an egg-shape with a smooth continuous edge

PENTAGON
a shape with five sides

HEXAGON
a shape with six sides

OCTAGON
a shape with eight sides

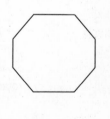

Arty Hearts

This is a simple paper-folding project that students can do with rectangular strips of paper. In fact, when you make a square from an $6\frac{1}{2}$ by 11-inch sheet of paper, the left-over strip is the right size for these hearts.

Materials Needed

page 10 (steps and pattern), rectangular strips of paper, about $6\frac{1}{2}$ x 2 inches (optional), scissors, crayons or markers

Math Concepts

shape, fractions, patterns, symmetry, angles, degrees, spatial relations, measurement

NCTM Standards

❖ understand numbers, ways of representing numbers, relationships among numbers, and number systems (*Number and Operations Standard 1.1*)

❖ analyze characteristics and properties of two- and three-dimensional geometric shapes, and develop mathematical arguments about geometric relationships (*Geometry Standard 3.1*)

❖ apply transformations and use symmetry to analyze mathematical situations (*Geometry Standard 3.3*)

❖ apply appropriate techniques, tools, and formulas to determine measurements (*Measurement Standard 4.2*)

Math Vocabulary:

rectangle	measurements
length	width
half	symmetry
pentagon	isosceles right triangle
line of symmetry	rotate
degrees	

Math Wise! Distribute copies of page 10. Use these tips to highlight math concepts and vocabulary for each step.

1 We are starting with a rectangle. When we give the measurements, we usually say the width and then the length. So that depends how we hold this rectangle. If we place it horizontally, like this, it is approximately $6\frac{1}{2}$ x 2 inches. How would we say the measurement if we rotated it vertically? $(2 \times 6\frac{1}{2}$ inches) This fold is called a book fold. Why do you think it has that name? We now have two equal, smaller rectangles. This middle line is called the "line of symmetry." That's because it divides two sides that are exactly the same.

2 Let's fold our top left edge down to meet our crease at the center. What was that crease called? (line of symmetry) Now we'll make a symmetrical fold, bringing the right corner down to make exactly the same fold that we made on the left side.

3 & 4 It looks like a tent, doesn't it? How many sides do we have now? (5) And what is this shape called? (pentagon) Let's flip it over. What does it look like now? (a house) The "roof" is an isosceles right triangle. Isosceles means that two sides are the same length. Right means that the triangle has a right angle that makes a perfect square corner and measures 90°. Now let's rotate it 180° (that's 90° twice), so that the roof is at the bottom. Fold each of the corners down, making four symmetrical triangles. Then flip it over again! You can write a message inside your heart.

Beyond the Folds!

❖ Distribute the Basic Geometric Shapes resource sheet on page 8. Have students identify different shapes during the process of the heart model (rectangle, triangle, pentagon). Can they find an example of each shape somewhere in the classroom?

❖ Show students how to turn a rectangular sheet of paper into a square. Fold down one top corner so that the top edge lines up with a side edge. Note that this forms two congruent triangles—in fact, two isosceles right triangles. Crease. Fold down the remaining strip at the bottom, crease well and tear off, or cut off the strip. That excess strip is the perfect dimension for a heart. Use the remaining square for another origami project.

❖ To provide hands-on practice with angle measurement, give each student a corner (right angle) from a piece of paper or cardstock. Have them test different corners in the room to see if they are true right angles. If the corner is not a perfect fit, ask them to determine whether it is greater or less than 90°. If students are ready to measure angles in degrees, you might introduce the terms acute and obtuse.

How to Make Hearts and Heart Pattern

1 Cut out a strip from the pattern below, placing it facedown, with the ★ in the top left corner. (Or cut out a $6\frac{1}{2}$ x 2-inch rectangular strip, and place it pattern side facedown.) Fold in half crosswise, right to left. Crease well and open.

2 Fold down the top left corner, so that the upper edge lies along the crease formed by the center fold. Follow the diagonal fold lines. Repeat with the other corner. Crease well and leave folded.

3 Flip the model over and rotate it so that the point is at the bottom. Then fold down each of the top four corners an equal amount, as shown.

4 Flip the model over again to reveal your heart shape! Repeat steps 1 through 3 with rectangular strips of different sizes.

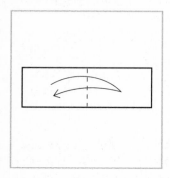 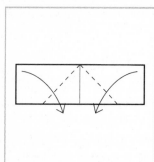 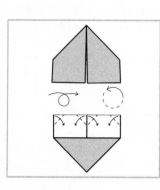 

Cut these three strips out to make three hearts of different sizes. Send one as a note to someone special!

Handy Envelope

Math Wise! Distribute copies of pages 12 and 13. Use these tips to highlight math concepts and vocabulary for each step.

Make this handy envelope from any rectangular piece of paper, or use the envelope pattern on page 13. Students can write a message on the inside, fold it up, address it, and send it.

Materials Needed

page 12 (steps), page 13 (pattern) or any rectangular sheet of paper, tape or a sticker, scissors

Math Concepts

shape, symmetry, fractions, area, measurement, multiplication

NCTM Standards

* understand meanings of operations and how they relate to one another (*Number and Operations Standard 1.2*)

* analyze characteristics and properties of two- and three-dimensional geometric shapes and develop mathematical arguments about geometric relationships (*Geometry Standard 3.1*)

* apply transformations and use symmetry to analyze mathematical situations (*Geometry Standard 3.3*)

* use visualization, spatial reasoning, and geometric modeling to solve problems (*Geometry Standard 3.4*)

* understand measurable attributes of objects and the units, systems, and processes of measurement (*Measurement Standard 4.2*)

Math Vocabulary

rectangle	width
length	area
line of symmetry	triangle
base	apex
height	bisect

1 What shape are we starting with? (a rectangle) **When we fold it, what shapes do we make?** (two smaller congruent rectangles) **What fraction of the large rectangle is one of the small rectangles?** ($\frac{1}{2}$) **We say the small rectangles are half the surface space, or area, of the large rectangle.**

The way we find the area of a rectangle is to multiply the width by the length. (Using the dimensions of the paper, have students find the area of the big rectangle.) **For the smaller rectangles, the width is now half as long as the big rectangle, but the length is the same. What do you think will happen to the area?** (It will be half that of the big rectangle.)

2 Origami folds are often very symmetrical, which means we make a fold that is exactly the same on each side. We're folding the bottom corners to meet the line of symmetry. Look at the two triangles we're forming. They are both isosceles right triangles. They have two sides the same and two angles the same. The other angle is a right angle, a perfect square corner.

3 The bottom of a triangle is called the base, and the top is called the apex. Our triangle here is upside down, so we're calling the top the base! We're folding the apex to a point above the base.

4 The part we're tucking in is a little triangle. Folding it like this cuts the height (from the base to the apex) about in half. The point should reach just about to the bottom.

5 With these folds, we are bisecting, or cutting in half, the small lower little triangles.

6 Again, we are folding the top corners down to the line of symmetry, forming more isosceles right triangles. This is a common origami shape.

7 Voila! An envelope. See the new rectangle we've formed.

Beyond the Folds!

* Show students how to find area by measuring the original rectangle's dimensions and multiplying length and width (6 x 8 inches). Now measure the completed envelope's dimensions and calculate that area. Help students master this skill by challenging them to measure and calculate the area of rectangles of different sizes. They might also explore the ratio between the folded and unfolded shapes.

* Open up a completed envelope and let students explore the shapes formed by all of the creases. Have them find shapes of equal dimensions.

How to Make the Envelope

1 Cut out the envelope pattern on page 13 and place it facedown with the ★ in the top left corner. Or use a rectangular sheet of paper, placing the side of the paper that will be the outside of your envelope facedown.

Write your message on the side that's facing up, leaving an empty border (as shown) around the edge. Fold the paper in half crosswise, left to right, so that the long edges meet. Crease, and unfold.

2 Fold up the bottom left corner so that the bottom edge meets the center crease line you just made. Repeat with the bottom right corner.

3 Fold up the bottom point along the fold line to meet a point above the base of the large triangle.

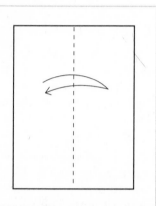
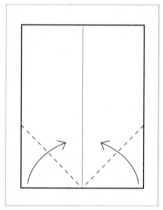
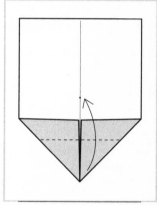

4 You have formed a new triangle. Tuck the point of that triangle under the horizontal edge. Crease well.

5 Fold in the left edge, cutting the little triangle at the bottom in half. Crease well and repeat with the right edge.

6 Fold down the top left corner to meet the center crease. Repeat with the top right corner.

7 Bring down the top point and tuck it into the bottom pocket. Crease the top edge, and seal with a sticker or piece of tape!

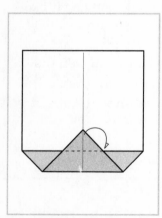
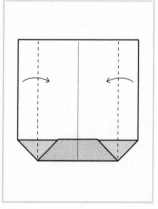
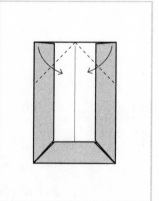
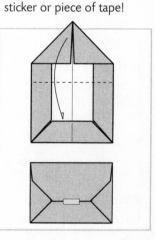
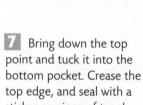

Envelope model created by Gay Merrill Gross and John Cunliffe.

Envelope Origami Pattern

Write a message on the back of this pattern. Then seal your message in its own envelope. Leave a border for the folded edges.

This side will be the outside of your envelope!

★

_____

_____

_____

_____ :From

To: _____

_____

_____

_____

_ _ _ _ _ _ _ _ _ _ _ _ _ _ _ _

Expanding Invitation

The secret of this model is to make sure to fold the first four steps in both directions, front and reverse, to make the crease very flexible. The final fold to create the form is tricky the first time, but becomes easy with practice. Fill the invitation with confetti to make your invitation a blast!

Materials Needed

page 15 (steps), page 16 (pattern) or a square sheet of paper (any dimension), scissors, crayons or markers, confetti (optional)

Math Concepts

fractions, size, symmetry, shape, multiplication, using coordinates on a grid

NCTM Standards

✖ compute fluently and make reasonable estimates *(Number and Operations Standard 1.3)*

✖ specify locations and describe spatial relationships using coordinate geometry and other representational systems *(Geometry Standard 3.2)*

✖ represent and analyze mathematical situations and structures using algebraic symbols *(Algebra Standard 2.2)*

✖ understand measurable attributes of objects and the units, systems, and processes of measurement *(Measurement Standard 4.1)*

Math Vocabulary

square	triangle
fractions	half
quarters	eighths
sixteenths	counterclockwise

Math Wise! Distribute copies of pages 15 and 16. Use these tips to highlight math concepts and vocabulary for each step.

1 We're starting with a square. For every fold, we need to reverse and make the fold backwards as well. Crease it sharply each time. That's because our finished model needs to have flexibility to fold in both directions to work properly.

2 We've divided the square into two equal rectangles. They are halves of our original square. Our next folds will divide the square into four equal parts, fourths or quarters.

3 We're going to make the same folds from the first two steps in the opposite direction, right to left. How many equal sections do we have? (8) What fraction does each section represent? $\left(\frac{1}{8}\right)$

4 Now we've cut each eighth in half, so there are twice as many sections. What fraction names each small square? $\left(\frac{1}{16}\right)$ How would we show the area of our square as an equation of square units? ($4 \times 4 = 16$) How would we show it as a division equation? ($16 \div 4 = 4$)

5 What fraction of our squares are covered by the triangles? $\left(\frac{9}{16}\right)$

6 & 7 We'll start with the bottom left corner and rotate counterclockwise, bringing each fold to the center line, under the previous corner. What fraction of our original square shows on the top? $\left(\frac{4}{16} \text{ or } \frac{1}{4}\right)$

Beyond the Folds!

✖ Express each step as a fraction: $\frac{1}{2}$, $\frac{1}{4}$, $\frac{1}{8}$, $\frac{1}{16}$. Open the completed, folded page and ask students to shade in different fractions ($\frac{2}{16}$, $\frac{3}{8}$, $\frac{5}{16}$, and so on). This will help them make concrete comparisons between equivalent fractions such as $\frac{2}{4}$ and $\frac{1}{2}$.

✖ Draw a grid on the board with numbers across and letters down: 1, 2, 3, 4 and A, B, C, D. Describe the squares on the invitation by their coordinates. Square B3, for example, would be in Row 2, Column 3. Make a game of shading in the squares with different colors, according to their coordinates.

How to Make the Invitation

1 Cut out the pattern on page 16, placing the square faceup with the ★ in the top right corner. Fold in half, top to bottom. Crease, unfold, reverse the fold, and unfold again.

2 Fold the bottom edge to meet the center fold line you just made. Crease well, open, and reverse the fold, creasing well again. Repeat with the top edge.

3 Now repeat step 1 in the opposite direction, folding the paper in half from left to right. Crease and unfold.

4 Now repeat step 2 in the opposite direction. Fold in the left edge to meet the center fold, and fold in the right to meet the center fold. With all of these creases, remember to crease well and reverse the fold.

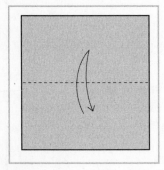 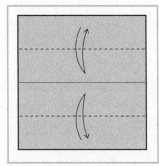 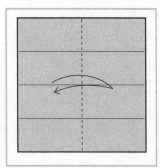 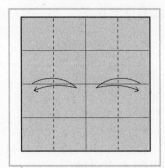

5 Fold the bottom left corner up to cover the third square in the second row. You are leaving the top row and the right column uncovered, and creating a triangle with the folded section. Crease well, and unfold. Now repeat with the other three corners. Note that you do not need to reverse these folds.

6 Pinch the dotted line that runs along the top of the bottom two squares on the right side. Then fold up this corner along the center line. Repeat with each dotted line so that the corners of the large square fold into a smaller square. Let each new fold slip under the last.

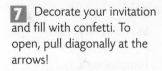

7 Decorate your invitation and fill with confetti. To open, pull diagonally at the arrows!

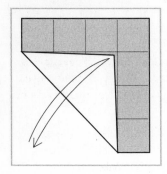 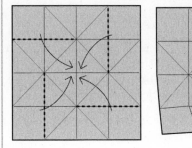 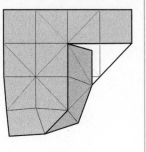 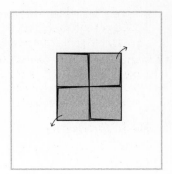

Invitation Pattern

Put some confetti in the middle of this invitation and watch it fly when the invitation is opened.

 It's important to reverse the folds, creasing back and forth with steps 1–4.
That will help all the sections fall into place when you make your final fold.

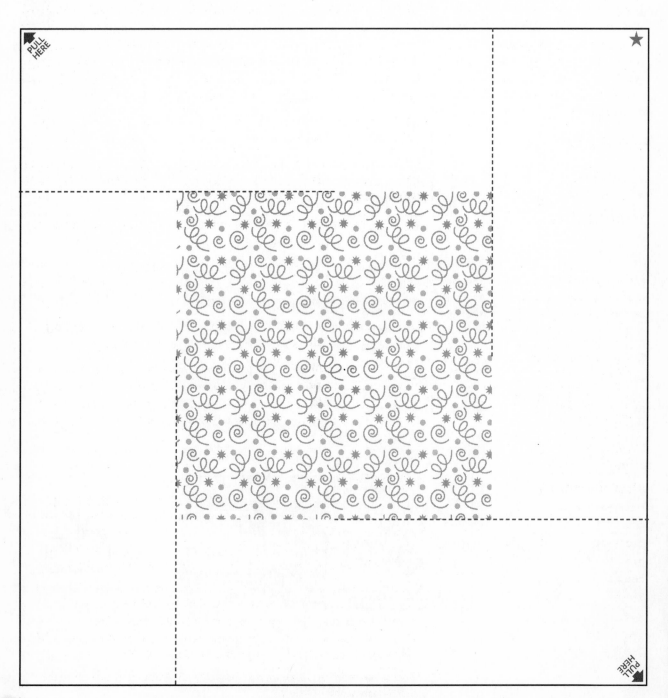

One-Snip Star

Math Wise! Distribute copies of pages 18 and 19. Use these tips to highlight math concepts and vocabulary for each step.

Ask students if they know how to make a perfect 5-pointed star with a piece of paper and one snip. Then teach them this simple method. They'll be glad to have the one-snip star in their bag of tricks!

Materials Needed

page 18 (steps), page 19 (pattern) or a $8\frac{1}{2}$ x 10-inch rectangle (or any rectangle of the same proportion), scissors

Math Concepts

shape, angles, fractions, symmetry, proportion

NCTM Standards

✳ understand numbers, ways of representing numbers, relationships among numbers, and number systems (*Number and Operations Standard 1.1*)

✳ understand meanings of operations and how they relate to one another (*Number and Operations Standard 1.2*)

✳ analyze change in various contexts (*Algebra Standard 2.1*)

✳ use visualization, spatial reasoning, and geometric modeling to solve problems (*Geometry Standard 3.4*)

Math Vocabulary

rectangle

ratio

trapezoid

half

quarter

eighth

bisect

quadrilateral

negative space

1 We're starting with a rectangle. It's not quite the standard $8\frac{1}{2}$ x 11-inch dimensions of a regular sheet of copy paper. It's smaller—$6\frac{3}{8}$ x $7\frac{1}{2}$ inches. You can use rectangles of other sizes, but they should have the same proportion or ratio as this one. In other words, you could make a large star with a $12\frac{1}{4}$ x 15-inch rectangle and it will work as well. We're folding it in half.

2 Now we're making quarters. But if we opened it up, we'd have eighths. That's because we have two layers.

3 This fold is a little tricky because we're folding it at an angle. The shape we just folded is a trapezoid. It has two parallel lines. Find them.

4 When we fold it back here, we're making an accordion fold. We're bisecting the angle, splitting it in half.

5 See how these shapes here are both irregular four-sided shapes, or quadrilaterals. It's hard to imagine how we're going to get a perfect star from these odd shapes.

6 Now we're making an accordion fold again. It's starting to look more uniform, with layers of the same shape.

7 & **8** We want to make an angle that's not too narrow, not too wide. Each point on your star will be twice the size of this snip. Let's unfold the piece we snipped and see! Look at the negative space—the star-shaped hole we left in the big piece.

Beyond the Folds!

✳ For a history connection, students may be interested to know that George Washington's original sketch for the United States flag included 6-pointed stars. Betsy Ross suggested 5-pointed stars, but the committee thought that would be too difficult to make. She took out a piece of paper and performed this little trick to demonstrate the ease of creating a perfect, symmetrical 5-pointed star.

✳ Have the class make enough stars to arrange on a big flag. Use red, white, and blue construction paper for the background and create the stars from white paper. Then examine the arrangement of the 50 stars that represent the states. They are staggered, and line up on the diagonals. Ask students how the total can be expressed as an algebraic equation: (5 x 6) + (4 x 5) = 30 + 20 = 50.

✳ Discuss the order of operations, and how the total would be different if the parentheses were not used.

How to Make a Star

1 Cut out the star pattern on page 19 and place it facedown with the ★ in the upper left corner. Or use an $8\frac{1}{2}$ x 10-inch rectangle, pattern side facedown. Fold the paper in half, bringing the top edge down to meet the bottom in a valley fold. Crease.

2 Fold in half again, bringing the right side over to meet the left. Crease, and unfold. Now bring the bottom edge up to meet the top. Crease, and unfold again.

3 Bring the top left corner down to meet the center horizontal fold line. Begin the fold at the center vertical line, as shown. The corner should meet the dot. Crease.

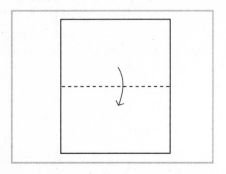

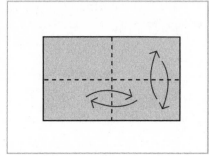

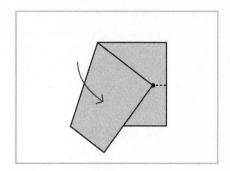

4 Now bring the top edge that you just folded back over to line up with the left edge, following the fold line. Crease well.

5 Fold over the top right corner along the fold line. Crease along the edge you just made below.

6 Fold back the left corner along the fold line so that the edges line up.

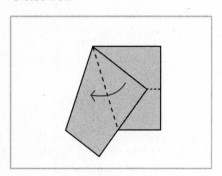

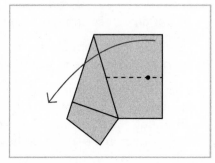

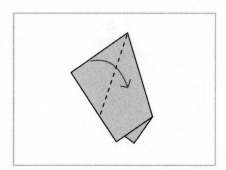

7 Make a snip at an angle, as shown.

8 Unfold the small piece you just snipped off to find your star!

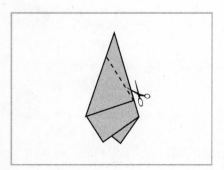

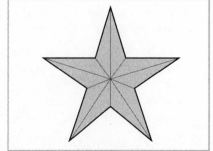

Star Pattern

Make a perfect 5-pointed star with nine folds and one snip!

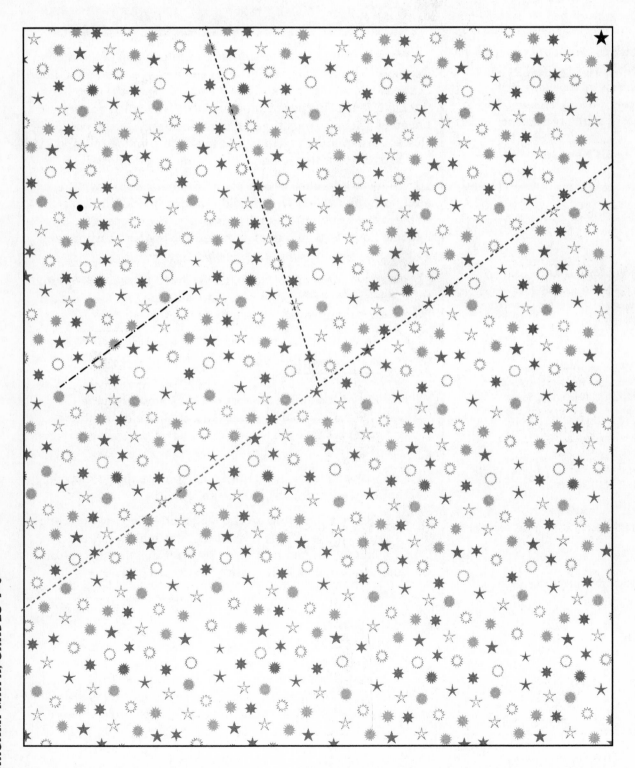

Twirly Copter

Make this excellent twirler with any square piece of paper. Launch it by throwing it bottom-side up, and watch its slow, spiraling descent.

Materials Needed

page 21 (steps), page 22 (pattern) or any square piece of paper, scissors, glue stick

Math Concepts

Shape, symmetry, fractions, spatial relations, measurement, speed, direction, velocity

NCTM Standards

- compute fluently and make reasonable estimates *(Number and Operations Standard 1.4)*
- analyze change in various contexts *(Algebra Standard 2.4)*
- analyze characteristics and properties of two- and three-dimensional geometric shapes, and develop mathematical arguments about geometric relationships *(Geometry Standard 3.1)*
- apply transformations and use symmetry to analyze mathematical situations *(Geometry Standard 3.3)*

Math Vocabulary

square
triangle
congruent
isosceles right triangle
line of symmetry
horizontal
vertical
degrees

Math Wise! Distribute copies of pages 21 and 22. Use these tips to highlight math concepts and vocabulary for each step.

1 We're putting our square down in the position of a diamond. Remember that a diamond is not really a shape. It's just a different way of looking at a square! After we make the two folds, we have four congruent triangles. They are called congruent because they are exactly equal in measurements; if we folded this square in fourths, we would lay each triangle on top of the others and their angles and sides would match perfectly.

2 We have two lines of symmetry. Shapes can be symmetrical along different lines. We are folding our top and bottom points to meet the horizontal line of symmetry. If we rotate it 90°, it becomes our vertical line of symmetry. Now let's turn it back so we can read the diagrams easily.

3 When we make multiple folds, we need to prevent the fold from "creeping." Hold it in place carefully as you fold and press. How many layers do we have now? (four)

4 Now how many layers do we have? (eight) How could you know that without counting? (We had four layers, and we just doubled them by folding them in half.)

5 This shape looks like a necktie. What kind of shape is it? (a hexagon) Once we fold it, what kind of shape do we have? (a pentagon) How did we get a five-sided shape from a six-sided one? (We gained one side with the folded edge, but lost two with the double layer.)

6 Fold just one layer at an angle, as you see in the picture. The angle is part of what will make it twirl.

7 & **8** Repeat that step on the other side. See how our angle is the same (congruent), only opposite? That makes the twirly copter symmetrical and balanced. Throw it up with the bottom-side up. What makes it flip over? (The bottom part is heavier.)

Beyond the Folds!

- Take a square of paper the same size as the square you used for the twirly copter. Ask students to do anything they want to it: crumple it in a ball; make a paper airplane, fold it however they'd like. Then ask them to explore the different aerodynamics of their creations. Which goes the farthest? The fastest? The most accurate? Encourage them to consider what properties influence the flight of the page.

How to Make the Twirly Copter

 TIP! Many problems in origami can crop up when you fold things in thick layers. One is that the folded edge itself takes up space. That makes it difficult to keep everything exactly the same size. It helps to press it as flat as you can at each step.

1 Cut out the twirly copter pattern on page 22 and place the square like a diamond, facedown with the ★ at the top. Or use a square sheet of paper, pattern side facedown. Fold in half, top to bottom, crease, and unfold. Repeat, folding in half, left to right.

2 Fold down the top point to meet the center point of the square. Crease. Repeat with the bottom point.

3 Fold down the top edge to meet the center fold line, and crease well. Repeat with the bottom edge.

4 Repeat this step again, folding the top and bottom edges in to meet the center fold line. Crease well, and press flat.

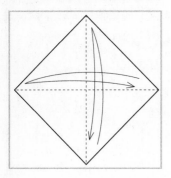
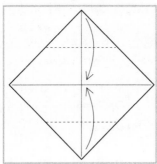
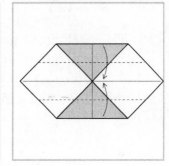
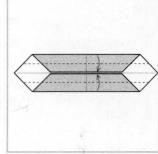

5 Turn over. Apply glue only at the center as shown. Fold over the right corner to meet the left corner, creasing and pressing flat to help the sides stick together.

6 Fold down the front flap at an angle, along the fold lines.

7 Repeat step 6, folding the back flap back.

8 Adjust the wings. To launch, throw with the handle pointing upward.

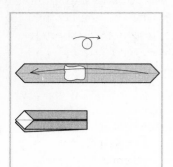

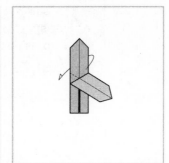

Twirly Copter Pattern

Throw this twirler up in the air with the bottom up, and watch it twirl all the way down.

Fancy Photo Frame

Students can make great holiday gifts with this simple foldable frame! Use it to highlight their photos and drawings.

Materials Needed

page 24 (steps), page 25 (pattern) or 6-inch square

Math Concepts

multiplication, fractions, patterns, shape, symmetry, angles, dimension, measurement

NCTM Standards

- understand meanings of operations and how they relate to one another *(Number and Operations Standard 1.2)*
- analyze characteristics and properties of two- and three-dimensional geometric shapes, and develop mathematical arguments about geometric relationships *(Geometry Standard 3.1)*
- apply transformations and use symmetry to analyze mathematical situations *(Geometry Standard 3.3)*
- understand measurable attributes of objects and the units, systems, and processes of measurement *(Measurement Standard 4.1)*
- apply appropriate techniques, tools, and formulas to determine measurements *(Measurement Standard 4.2)*

Math Vocabulary

equation	divide
multiply	half
quarter	perpendicular
right angle	isosceles right triangle
square	fractions

Math Wise! Distribute copies of pages 24 and 25. Use these tips to highlight math concepts and vocabulary for each step.

1 Let's see if I can express this first fold with an equation. When I fold the paper, it's one square divided into two equal parts, $1 \div 2 = \frac{1}{2}$. Now when I unfold it, I can say it's one square times two equal parts, $1 \times 2 = 2$. What shape are the halves? (rectangles) With our second fold, we've divided the square into quarters, or four equal parts. What shape are the quarters? (squares) Our two center fold lines are perpendicular to each other, meaning that they intersect or cross at right angles. See how they create four corner angles of 90°?

2 Now we have four isosceles right triangles—triangles with two congruent sides around a 90° angle. Together, these four triangles make another square. This square is also divided into quarters, just in a different way.

3 Wait a second before we flip it over! Think about the steps we've done and try to imagine what the back will look like. Now flip it! Is it as you pictured it, another smaller square?

4 When we make these two folds and divide up the square like we did in step one, what do we call the four equal parts? (quarters) We have four triangles making up our square again. But each of those triangles is made up of two smaller triangles. Write an equation that tells us how many triangles we have. ($4 \times 2 = 8$; each of four triangles is divided in half) We have eight triangles altogether. So what fraction of the square does each triangle take up? (one eighth)

5 Picture it again before we flip it over. OK, now we're folding one layer of each square back. And we're left with a square within a square!

6 We can make the frame stand up by folding two opposite flaps out so that they are perpendicular to the frame. What angle will you make when you pull the flap out perpendicular to the back of the frame? (90° or right angle)

Beyond the Folds!

- Have students use a ruler to measure the inside square of the frame and cut their picture to a slightly larger square that will fit nicely in the frame. If they don't have a photo handy, have them measure a piece of paper and cut it to the right size. (They may need to test whether it fits properly and trim as needed.) Invite them to write a message or draw a picture to insert in their frame. They can replace it later with a photograph.

How to Make the Frame

1 Use the frame pattern on page 25 and place the page faceup, with the ★ in the upper right corner. Or use a 6-inch square, pattern side face up. Fold the page in half, top to bottom, crease, and unfold. Then repeat, folding in half from right to left. Crease and unfold.

2 Fold in each corner to meet the center point. Crease well.

3 Flip over and position like a diamond.

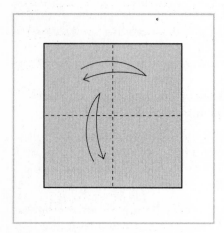

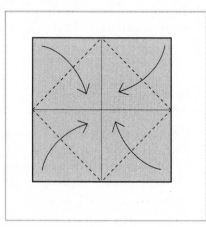

4 Again, fold each corner in to meet the center point. Crease well. Flip over.

5 Fold back each corner from the center to meet the outside corner. Crease well.

6 This is your completed picture frame. Tuck a favorite picture in the frame. To make the frame stand up, fold out one flap on the back to create the base or two of the flaps that are opposite each other to create sides.

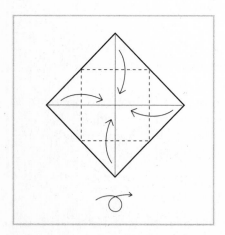

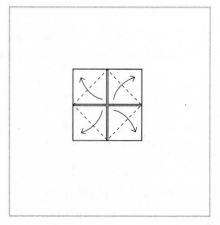

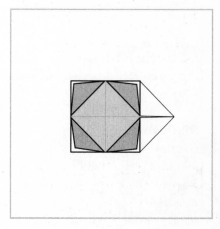

ORIGAMI MATH, GRADES 4–6

Frame Pattern

Put a favorite photo or a drawing in your own handmade frame.

Math Fortune Teller

This timeless paper game has a mathematical twist!

Materials Needed

page 27 (steps), page 28 (pattern) or square piece of paper, crayons or markers

Math Concepts

shapes, patterns, symmetry, spatial relations, probability, angles

NCTM Standards

✂ understand numbers, ways of representing numbers, relationships among numbers, and number systems (*Number and Operations Standard 1.1*)

✂ understand meanings of operations and how they relate to one another (*Number and Operations Standard 1.2*)

✂ understand patterns, relations, and functions (*Algebra Standard 2.1*)

✂ represent and analyze mathematical situations and structures using algebraic symbols (*Algebra Standard 2.2*)

✂ apply transformations and use symmetry to analyze mathematical situations (*Geometry Standard 3.3*)

Math Vocabulary

square

quadrilateral

diagonal

line of symmetry

triangle

isosceles right triangle

bisect

Math Wise! Distribute copies of pages 27 and 28. Use these tips to highlight math concepts and vocabulary for each step.

1 **What shape are we starting with?** (a square—a quadrilateral, or four-sided figure) **What makes this shape a square?** (The four sides are all congruent or equal in length and there are four right angles.) **We've created a diagonal line of symmetry. What shapes do we have now?** (two triangles) **Notice that they both have two congruent sides forming a right or 90° angle. What kind of triangles are they?** (isosceles right triangles)

2 **Our fold lines make a giant "X." We have two lines of symmetry. How many matching sections do we have?** (four) **What shapes are they?** (triangles) **How are these angles like and unlike the big triangles we made in step one?** (They are smaller in size, but they are also isosceles right triangles.)

3 **Now we have four smaller isosceles right triangles. Together they make one smaller square. And our lines of symmetry are the same—only shorter!**

4 **In this step, we're making it smaller again! We have four small isosceles right triangles—but look closely! It's really eight triangles. Do you notice what happens each time we bisect, or divide, one of these isosceles right triangles in half evenly?** (We get another smaller isosceles right triangle.)

5 **This time we're not folding on the diagonal. We're folding on the horizontal and vertical lines of symmetry!**

6 **We have four fortunes on the inside. What are the chances that your friend will get one particular fortune?** (One in four, or $\frac{1}{4}$. Although there are eight panels on the inside, two of each lead to the same fortune.)

Beyond the Folds!

✂ Show students how the fraction in step 6 reduces: It's two chances in eight, or $\frac{2}{8} = \frac{1}{4}$.

✂ Students can make their own fortune tellers from any square piece of paper. Have them make up their own sets of math equations to use in their fortune tellers.

✂ Have students keep track of how many times certain fortunes come up. See if their probability prediction proves true.

How to Make a Fortune Teller

1 Cut out the pattern on page 28 and place the paper facedown, with the ★ in the top left corner. Or use any square piece of paper, pattern side facedown. Fold in half along the diagonal, so that the bottom left corner meets the top right corner. Crease well. Unfold.

2 Fold in half along the other diagonal, so that the bottom right and top left corners meet. Crease and unfold again.

3 Fold one corner to the center point. Crease well. Repeat with the other three corners.

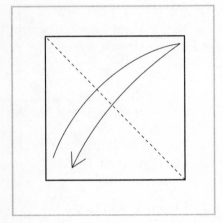

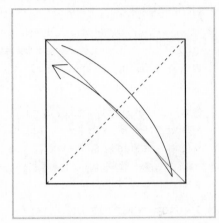

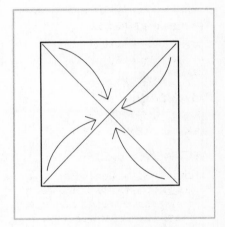

4 Flip over. Fold each corner to meet the center point again, creasing well with each fold.

5 Fold the square in half one way. Open it up and fold it in half the other way.

6 While it's still folded, stick your thumbs and index fingers into the four pockets at the bottom. Push the corners together and apart in different directions.

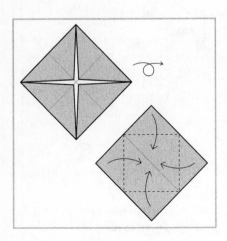

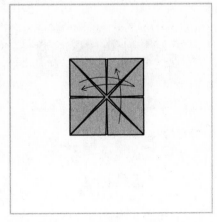

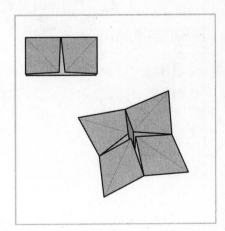

Fortune Teller Pattern

What's your math fortune? Fold this fortune teller to see what the numbers hold!

To play with the fortune teller: Hold the fortune teller closed. Have your friend point to an equation and give the answer. If he or she answers correctly, open the fortune teller in alternate directions, counting up to that number. Then have your friend pick an equation on a triangle inside the teller. Repeat the process and have your friend point to another triangle. Open it up, and read the math fortune to your friend!

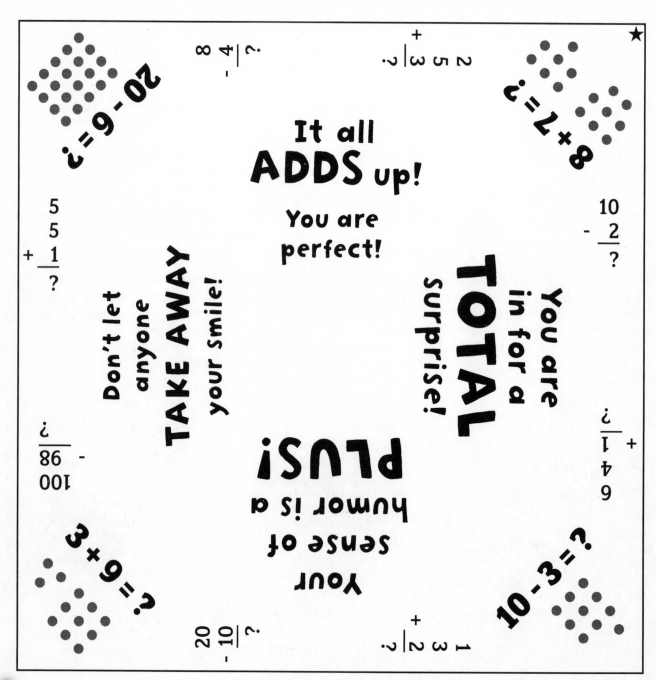

Tumbling Toy

This classic origami toy has a hidden mechanism that makes it tumble—extra weight on one side. Show students a model before they make the toy and see if they can guess how it works.

Materials Needed

page 30 (steps), page 31 (pattern) or square piece of paper (thin paper works best), scissors, markers or crayons

Math Concepts

Fractions, spatial relations, shape, speed

NCTM Standards

❊ understand patterns, relations, and functions (*Algebra Standard 2.1*)

❊ analyze characteristics and properties of two- and three-dimensional geometric shapes, and develop mathematical arguments about geometric relationships (*Geometry Standard 3.1*)

❊ apply transformations and use symmetry to analyze mathematical situations (*Geometry Standard 3.3*)

❊ understand measurable attributes of objects and the units, systems, and processes of measurement (*Measurement Standard 4.1*)

Math Vocabulary

square
rectangle
horizontal
vertical
diagonal
half
quarter
asymmetry

Math Wise! Distribute copies of pages 30 and 31. Use these tips to highlight math concepts and vocabulary for each step.

1 We're folding our square in half to form two rectangles, and then opening it. How many ways can you fold a square paper in half? (four: horizontally, vertically, and along both diagonals)

2 We're folding it into quarters. But we're leaving one side folded and opening the other. It's now asymmetrical. That will become important to the way this toy works. Another way to express the folds would be with this equation: $\frac{1}{4} + \frac{1}{4} + \frac{2}{4} = \frac{4}{4} = 1$.

3 Which folds are easier to make: the top or the bottom corners? (the top) Why? (because the bottom layer is thicker; you are folding more layers)

4 What shape are we starting with on this step? (an octagon) What familiar object is an octagon? (a stop sign)

5 When you make this fold, there is a natural place to make the crease. Why does the paper seem to want to fold here? (There are hidden layers underneath that end there.)

6 Set the tumbler up with the extra folded edge at the top. Give it a little push. What makes the tumbler tumble? (The extra layers add extra weight to the edge.)

Beyond the Folds!

❊ Try tumbling the tumbler on an inclined plane. What happens? Encourage the students to make tumblers of different sizes and with different kinds of paper to see what has the best action.

❊ Ask students to look at home for examples of other toys and mechanisms that work because of the way they are weighted. Make a science connection and discuss the effects of gravity.

How to Make a Tumbling Toy

1 Cut out the pattern on page 31 and place it facedown with the ★ in the upper left corner. Or use any square piece of paper, pattern side facedown. Fold in half, top to bottom. Crease and unfold.

2 Fold the top and bottom edges in to meet the center crease. Crease well, and unfold the top edge only. Leave the bottom edge folded up.

3 Fold in the top corners to meet the quarter crease line. Fold the bottom corners up to meet the raw edge of the fold at the center.

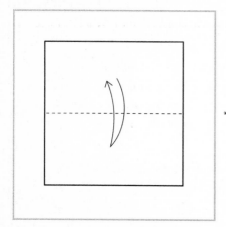

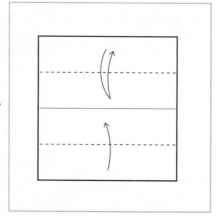

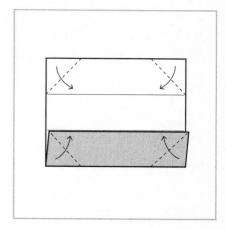

4 Fold the top edge down to meet the quarter crease. Fold the bottom edge up to meet the raw folded edge.

5 Fold the short edges toward the center. You can use the fold lines and the hidden edges underneath as a guide.

6 Open the short edges 90°. Set your tumbler upright. One edge has extra folds. Place this edge at the top. Then give a light tap and watch it tumble.

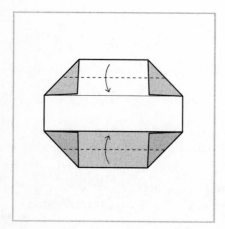

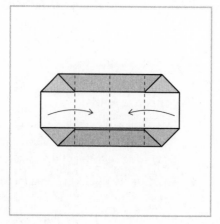

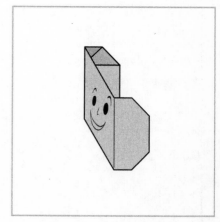

Tumbling Toy Pattern

Can you figure out the trick that makes this toy tumble over? It's all in the folds!

Paper Magic

Hold up an $8\frac{1}{2}$ x 11-inch sheet of paper and ask students if they think you can cut a hole big enough for them to fit through. Then amaze them with this simple trick.

Materials Needed

page 33 (steps), page 34 (pattern) or any rectangular sheet of paper, scissors

Math Concepts

spatial relations, pattern, topology, size, dimension, measurement, perimeter, area

NCTM Standards

✴ analyze change in various contexts *(Algebra Standard 2.4)*

✴ analyze characteristics and properties of two- and three-dimensional geometric shapes, and develop mathematical arguments about geometric relationships *(Geometry Standard 3.1)*

✴ apply transformations and use symmetry to analyze mathematical situations *(Geometry Standard 3.3)*

✴ use visualization, spatial reasoning, and geometric modeling to solve problems *(Geometry Standard 3.4)*

Math Vocabulary

alternating

edge

perimeter

area

1 It's hard to imagine how you could cut a huge hole out of this size paper, isn't it? How might folding it in half before we make cuts help? (By folding the paper in half and cutting, you're making cuts that are twice as long.)

2 We're cutting lines in an alternating pattern—first from one edge and then from the other. Can you think of other patterns that alternate? (Answers might include mathematical patterns such as odd and even numbers, visual patterns such as a checkerboard, physical patterns in which body weight shifts from right to left as in walking, or even sound patterns with alternating sounds or beats.)

3 The instructions tell us not to cut through the top and bottom edge as we cut along the fold line. Why do you think this is? (The top and bottom edge hold together the strip of paper that will form the circle.)

4 Was it magic? Not really. We simply turned the entire surface area of a page into the perimeter, or edge of a circle. That's why we can have such a big hole.

Beyond the Folds!

✴ Show students the classic Mobius strip model. That is another form that plays with the concept of beginning and end, inside and out. Students can learn how to make a Mobius strip at the website for Zoom: http://pbskids.org/zoom/phenom/mobiusstrip.html.

✴ Ask students to measure the perimeter and the area of the original page. Then ask them to measure the perimeter of the new shape. How do they compare? Note that the original perimeter of the pattern on page 34 is 29 inches. But, when it's cut, the inside area has all become part of a much larger external edge. So the new perimeter is much greater, measuring more than 6 feet!

How to Make Paper Magic

1 Cut out the pattern on page 34 and place it facedown with the ★ in the upper left corner. Or use any $8\frac{1}{2}$ x 11-inch sheet of paper, pattern side facedown. Fold right to left, so that the right edge lines up with the left, and crease well.

2 Starting from the fold, cut alternating horizontal lines, being careful not to snip all the way through to the opposite edge. Follow the cut lines marked.

3 Now snip along the folded edge at the center. Start at your first cut line and snip along until you reach your last cut line. Again, be careful to leave the top and bottom edges of the paper uncut.

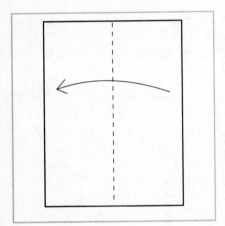
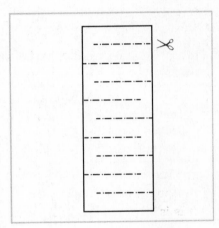
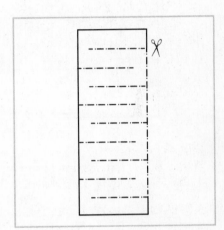

4 Open up the paper to reveal a large loop with a giant hole! You can carefully slip it over your arms, slide it to the ground, and step over it!

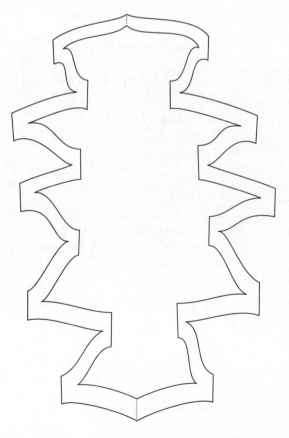

Paper Magic Pattern

Tell someone that you can walk through a piece of paper.
When they bet you can't, show them this trick.

★

Swimming Swan

These swans can be used as table decorations at a class party where they can float in a basin or fishbowl. Spread a little shortening on the bottom to protect the paper from getting wet and watch the swans swim!

Materials Needed

page 36 (steps), page 37 (pattern) or 6-inch square, pencil, scissors, shortening (optional)

Math Concepts

fractions, spatial relations, symmetry, shape, angles

NCTM Standards

- understand numbers, ways of representing numbers, relationships among numbers, and number systems *(Number and Operations Standard 1.1)*
- compute fluently and make reasonable estimates *(Number and Operations Standard 1.3)*
- analyze change in various contexts *(Algebra Standard 2.4)*
- analyze characteristics and properties of two- and three-dimensional geometric shapes, and develop mathematical arguments about geometric relationships *(Geometry Standard 3.1)*
- use visualization, spatial reasoning, and geometric modeling to solve problems *(Geometry Standard 3.4)*

Math Vocabulary

vertical	diagonal
bisect	congruent
half	thirds
acute	obtuse

Math Wise! Distribute copies of pages 36 and 37. Use these tips to highlight math concepts and vocabulary for each step.

1 We've positioned the square like a diamond. What direction is our fold line? (vertical) Suppose we positioned it like a square. What direction is our fold line? (a diagonal)

2 Now we are bisecting the angles below. What did we do when we bisected the angles? (cut them in half to form two congruent triangles) How many angles are under the folds at the bottom point? (four) Are they congruent or not? (yes) Why? (The first two triangles were congruent. When we bisected them, that doubled the number of angles but kept them congruent.)

3 & **4** When we flip it over, our model looks like a kite. How are the folds in this step like the last step and how are they different? (We're bisecting the angles again, which creates twice as many congruent angles. This time, there are eight angles at the tip.)

5 See this center line? Let's mark two points to show where the line divides into thirds. We want to make our fold line right at the top third. Then the point will meet the second third.

6 Notice how we're using the line of symmetry to fold the entire model in half evenly.

7 Here we change the bottom angle, to bring the neck up.

8 & **9** Now we're changing the angle at the base of the head. In these last two steps, did the angles we changed become more acute (narrow) or more obtuse (wide)? (obtuse)

Beyond the Folds!

- If students have the necessary math skills, have them estimate the number of degrees the angles changed in steps 6 and 7 and then use a protractor to check their answers.
- Have students work in groups and make swans of different sizes. Then have them arrange the swans to make a mobile. How does the size of the swans affect the balance of the mobile? (The larger ones weigh more and the mobile has to be adjusted accordingly.)
- Ask students to open up a completed swan and press the paper flat. How many different shapes can they see? How many triangles? Have them try to find shapes that exactly match each other and shade them with matching colors.

How to Make a Swan

1 Cut out the pattern on page 37 and place the page like a diamond, facedown with the ★ at the top point. Or use a 6-inch square, pattern side facedown. Fold in half so that the left point meets the right point. Crease and unfold.

2 Fold the lower left edge to meet the center crease. Crease. Repeat with the right side. Crease sharply. These two folds should line up at the center like a cone and meet at a sharp point at the bottom.

3 Turn over. Again, fold the long edges to the center. Try to keep the point crisp.

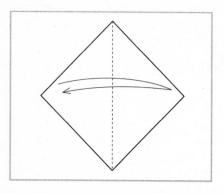

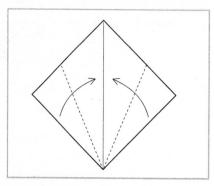

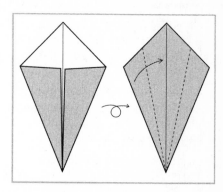

4 Fold up the bottom point to the top. Crease well.

5 Fold down the top point to the dot shown and crease.

6 Mountain fold the body in half along the center crease. The head should also fold in half.

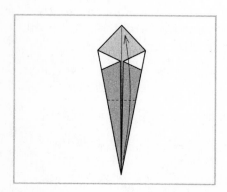

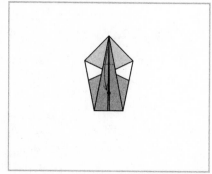

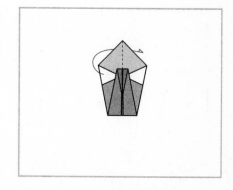

7 Lift the head and neck up, away from the body as shown. Crease the base of the neck again to set the new angle.

8 Holding the neck in place, bring the beak up. Crease the base of the head again to set the new angle.

9 Decorate your swan and set it afloat in water. Or make a set of swans to use as place cards.

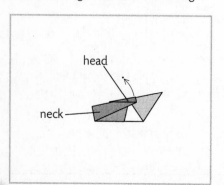

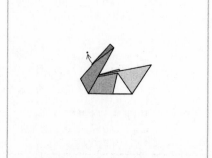

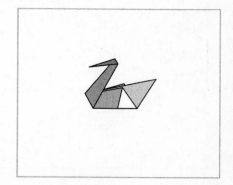

Swan Pattern

Add a special touch to a table setting by using origami swans for place cards.

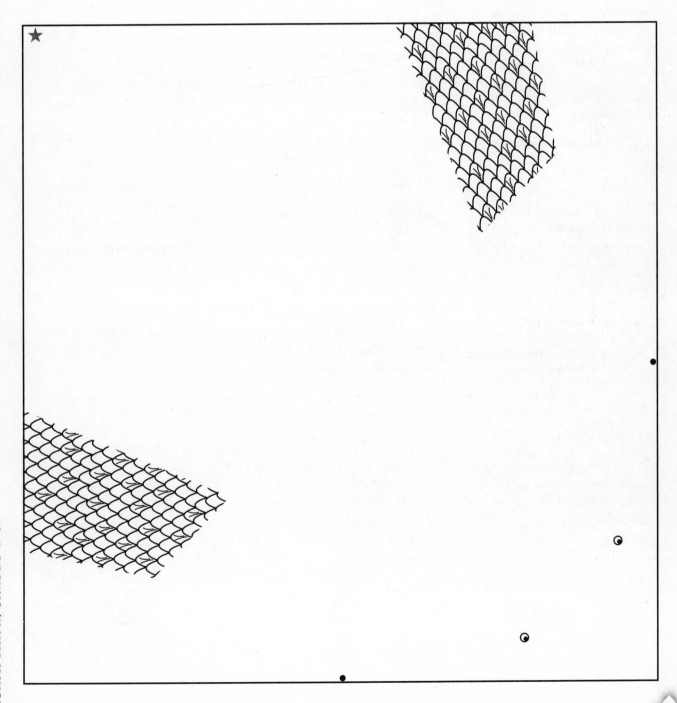

Kaleidoscope Pinwheel

This is a very simple form of what is sometimes called modular origami. Modular origami is made by connecting multiple pieces with the same folds.

Materials Needed

page 39 (steps), page 40 (pattern) or eight 2-inch squares, scissors, glue, construction paper (optional)

Math Concepts

fractions, patterns, symmetry, shape, addition, multiplication, area

NCTM Standards

- understand numbers, ways of representing numbers, relationships among numbers, and number systems *(Number and Operations Standard 1.1)*
- understand meanings of operations and how they relate to one another *(Number and Operations Standard 1.2)*
- analyze characteristics and properties of two- and three-dimensional geometric shapes and develop mathematical arguments about geometric relationships *(Geometry Standard 3.1)*
- apply transformations and use symmetry to analyze mathematical situations *(Geometry Standard 3.3)*
- use visualization, spatial reasoning, and geometric modeling to solve problems *(Geometry Standard 3.4)*

Math Vocabulary

square	quarter
diamond	multiply
square inches	point
counterclockwise	alternating

Math Wise! Distribute copies of pages 39 and 40. Use these tips to highlight math concepts and vocabulary for each step.

1 We're starting with a 2-inch square. What is the perimeter of the square? (8 inches) What is the area? (4 square inches) What is the perimeter of one of the new rectangles? (6 inches) What is the area? (2 square inches)

2 Now we're folding it in quarters. We have four layers of squares. What is the area of each square? (1 square inch) Now we're making seven more squares using the same folds. How many square inches of paper will we have in all? How can we show that as an equation? (4 sq. inches x 8 = 32 sq. inches)

3 Add the glue at the point that was in the center of the square. We want to keep the folds facing the same exact way for each square, so that they will all slide together properly.

4 For the second square, pick one with a different pattern from the first square. Notice how we attach the squares in a diamond position, with the raw edges facing out.

5 Each time we add a square, we'll switch patterns, so that the pinwheel pattern alternates. With each new square you attach, try to keep the same angle and move in the same direction, counterclockwise.

Beyond the Folds!

- Once students have arranged their Kaleidoscope Pinwheels, have them add a dab of glue to the back and attach it to a card. Before they make the card, have them calculate how big the card needs to be to mount the pinwheel. Then they should double that size to make a folded card.
- Help students figure out what the internal angles on the pinwheel are. Because all of the angles form a circle, we know that the total is 360°. We know that there are 8 angles and that they are equal. Therefore, each angle should be 45°. Show them 45° by folding a right angle in half. Let them use this as their guide.

How to Make a Kaleidoscope Pinwheel

1 Cut out the eight 2-inch squares from the kaleidoscope pattern on page 40, or cut out eight 2-inch squares from your own paper. Place the first square facedown. Fold in half bottom to top, and crease well.

2 Fold over the right side to meet the left. Repeat these steps with all eight squares.

3 Put a dab of glue in the corner that was the center point of the original square. Place the glue on the top layer.

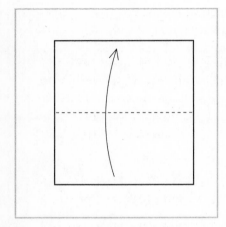

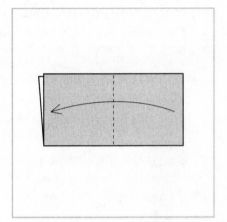

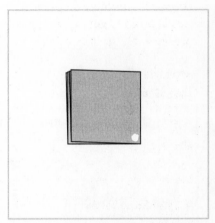

4 Slide the square with the glue on it into another square, as shown. Alternate between the two patterns as you add each square.

5 Now apply a dab of glue to the inside corner of the top square, and slide it into a third square. Repeat until you have an entire circle. Use the glue stick lightly.

6 Adjust the squares until they line up evenly to create a perfect array! Glue the pinwheel to a card or journal for decoration.

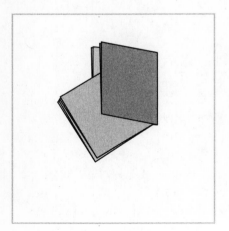

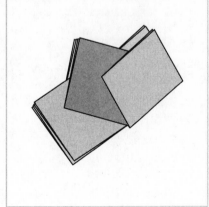

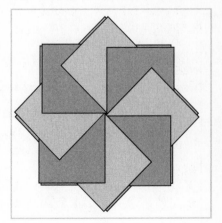

Kaleidoscope Pinwheel Pattern

This pinwheel is made from two very basic folds. Just repeat those folds on eight different squares and put them together to create a pinwheel with alternating colors or patterns. For a more colorful pattern, use colored pencils to decorate your squares before folding. Or create your own pattern using the blank backs of the squares. Paste your pinwheel to the front of a blank card to make a unique, handmade gift for someone special.

TIP! For the pinwheel to look good, you'll need to adjust the arrangement of the squares to make them line up. They need to be inserted at the same angles.

Little Box

Math Wise! Distribute copies of pages 42 and 43. Use these tips to highlight math concepts and vocabulary for each step.

This pattern offers students a good challenge and creates an elegant design. You can make a lid with a slightly bigger piece of paper. Or, using the same size paper, you can "cheat" on the folds, not folding them quite in to the center on steps 2 and 6, to produce a lid that is bigger than the box.

1 We're taking a square again, placing it like a diamond, and folding into quarters. A lot of models start this way.

2 We now have three parallel lines.

3 Here we have a shape with six sides. What is that called? (hexagon) When we fold it, we create a five-sided shape. What is that called? (pentagon) What happened when we folded it that caused the number of sides to go from six to five? (When the shape was folded on the line of symmetry, we folded up the bottom point, "hiding" the two lines on either side of the point. At the same time we "lost" those two lines, we gained a base line where the fold is.)

4 We're folding a little triangle here. How could you show that the upper triangle is twice the size of the lower triangle? (You can fit exactly two of the lower triangles in the space of the upper triangle.)

5 & **6** This fold is sometimes called a squash-fold. Now we've made another triangle that's twice the size of the small one—the same size as the bigger triangle.

7 See how this diagram shows the same folds that we made in step 2. But we're working with a smaller square, with more layers. So it's a harder fold to make. Make sure to crease it well.

8 This fold is sometimes called a reverse fold. We take a fold that already exists, from the step before, and turning it inside out!

9 This is like turning the pages of a book.

10 We're making these folds at the base of the top triangle. Grease it well here; these folds will become the top creases of our boxes.

11 & **12** Now we're folding at the base of the bottom triangle. Crease this well; it will form the bottom edges of our box.

Materials Needed

page 42 (steps), page 43 (pattern) or a 6-inch square, scissors

Math Concepts

fractions, spatial relationships, size, shape, volume, symmetry

NCTM Standards

✖ compute fluently and make reasonable estimates *(Number and Operations Standard 1.3)*

✖ understand patterns, relations, and functions *(Algebra Standard 2.1)*

✖ analyze characteristics and properties of two- and three-dimensional geometric shapes, and develop mathematical arguments about geometric relationships *(Geometry Standard 3.1)*

✖ use visualization, spatial reasoning, and geometric modeling to solve problems *(Geometry Standard 3.4)*

Math Vocabulary

square
diamond
quarters
parallel
hexagon
pentagon
triangle

Beyond the Folds!

✖ Have students make a lid with a slightly bigger piece of paper. If the bottom is a 6-inch square, they might make the lid from a $6\frac{1}{2}$-inch square.

✖ Before they begin, have students look at their square paper and estimate how many paper clips the box will hold. Have them revise their estimate when it is folded. Then let them test their estimates by filling their boxes with paper clips while keeping count! (They may use candies, pennies, or other small objects that are fun to count.)

✖ Challenge students to make a set of nesting boxes! Encourage them to start by making paper squares that are graduated in size by an exact measurement, such as a $\frac{1}{2}$-square-inch or 1-square-inch difference in sizes.

How to Make a Box

1 Cut out the box pattern on page 43, and place the square like a diamond facedown with the ★ at the top point. Or use a 6-inch square, pattern side facedown. Fold in half, bottom to top. Crease and unfold. Repeat, folding right to left. Crease and unfold.

2 Fold the left point to meet the center crease. Crease. Repeat, bringing the right point to the center line.

3 Bring the bottom point up to meet the top point, and crease.

4 Fold up the bottom left corner to meet the center fold. Crease, and unfold.

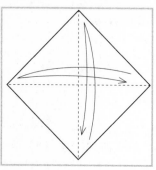
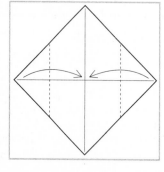
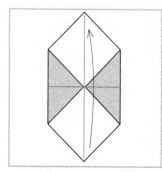
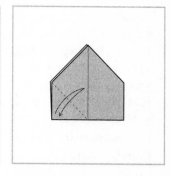

5 Stick your finger in between the two layers at the left. Push up the bottom edge to meet the center fold inside. Press open the triangle to complete the squash fold.

6 Flip over and make the same fold on the other side, pushing the bottom left point into the center of the square.

7 Fold the left corner (both layers) over to meet the center line. Crease and unfold. Repeat with the right corner.

8 Take the left corner, front layer only, and reverse-fold it inside. You are tucking the fold inside. Do the same with the right corner. Turn over and repeat with the two corners on the other side.

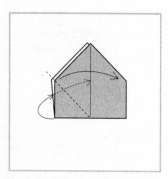
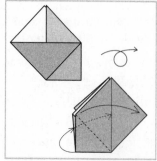
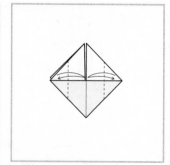
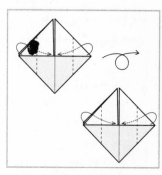

9 Fold the right flap over to the left side. Flip over and repeat.

10 Fold down the top corners into the center. They should tuck all the way in, down to the bottom point.

11 Fold the bottom point up to make a crease line for the bottom of the box. Unfold.

12 Insert finger in the top of the box and open. Adjust creases to make the box edges crisp.

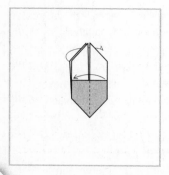
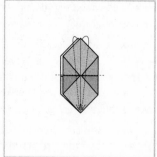
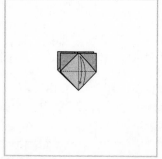
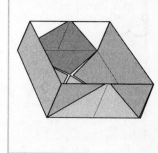

ORIGAMI MATH, GRADES 4–6

Box Pattern

Repeat this with a slightly larger square to make a lid.

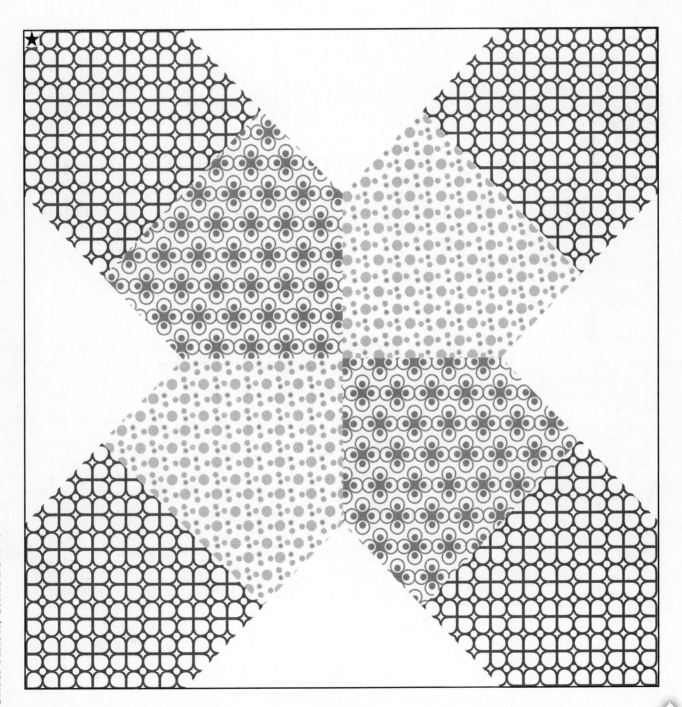

Incredible, Inflatable Cube

This two-dimensional object becomes a three-dimensional form when you fill it with an important ingredient: air!

Materials Needed

page 45 (steps), page 46 (pattern) or a 6-inch square, scissors

Note: light-weight paper works best for this pattern.

Math Concepts

spatial relations, area, volume, shape

NCTM Standards

✄ compute fluently and make reasonable estimates (*Number and Operations Standard 1.3*)

✄ understand patterns, relations, and functions (*Algebra Standard 2.1*)

✄ analyze characteristics and properties of two- and three-dimensional geometric shapes, and develop mathematical arguments about geometric relationships (*Geometry Standard 3.1*)

✄ use visualization, spatial reasoning, and geometric modeling to solve problems (*Geometry Standard 3.4*)

Math Vocabulary

horizontal	line of symmetry
vertical	trapezoid
parallel	parallelogram
isosceles right triangle	square
hexagon	bisect
apex	hypotenuse
cube	volume

Math Wise! Distribute copies of pages 45 and 46. Use these tips to highlight math concepts and vocabulary for each step.

1 We're creating a horizontal line of symmetry.

2 Now we have four layers of squares. If we open it up, how many lines of symmetry do we have? (two: horizontal and vertical)

3 This shape is a trapezoid. Which two lines are parallel? (the top and bottom) **What would we need to do to change this into a parallelogram?** (make the left and right edges parallel)

4 Now we have two isosceles right triangles. If we could put them together, what shape could we make? (a square)

5 Now we're creating four equal triangles. The two on the front form a square. Could you arrange all four to make a square? (yes, with all four top points facing in)

6 Now we're making a new shape with the top layer. What shape is it? (a hexagon)

7 We're bisecting these little triangles.

8 We're bringing the apex of the smaller triangle over to meet the hypotenuse of the larger triangle.

9 The air is what gives our cube its volume!

Beyond the Folds!

✄ Fill the cube with grains of uncooked rice and then tape the holes to make music shakers. How many grains of rice make the best sound?

✄ Help students calculate the volume of their cubes. Use this formula to help.

Volume = length x width x height

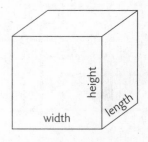

How to Make a Cube

1 Cut out the pattern on page 46 and place it with the ★ in the upper, left corner facedown. Or use a 6-inch square, pattern side facedown. Fold in half, bringing the top edge down to meet the bottom. Crease well.

2 Bring the right edge over to meet the left and crease well again.

3 Put your finger in between the top two layers on the left side and make a squash fold, pressing the upper left corner in and down to meet the lower right corner. This creates a shape that is a square on the left and a triangle on the right.

4 Flip over and repeat step 3, from the right.

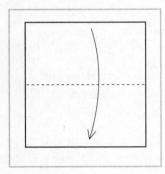 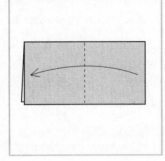 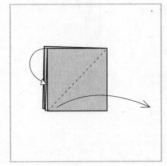 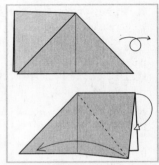

5 Fold up the bottom left corner, top layer only, to the top point. Crease. Repeat with the other three corners.

6 Fold in the left corner, top layer only, to meet the center crease. Crease. Repeat with right corner.

7 Fold down the front two triangles along the center fold to the center.

8 Fold those same triangles again, so that the point tucks down into the triangle pockets completely. Crease again.

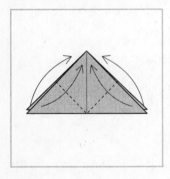  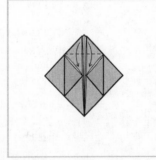 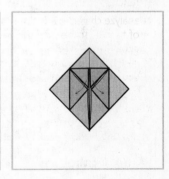

9 Flip over. Repeat steps 6–8 on the back side.

10 Blow through the hole at the bottom to inflate your cube!

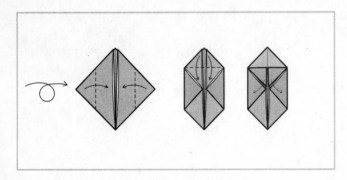 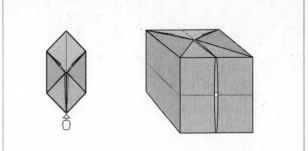

Cube Pattern

You have to blow air in this "balloon" to turn it into a cube.

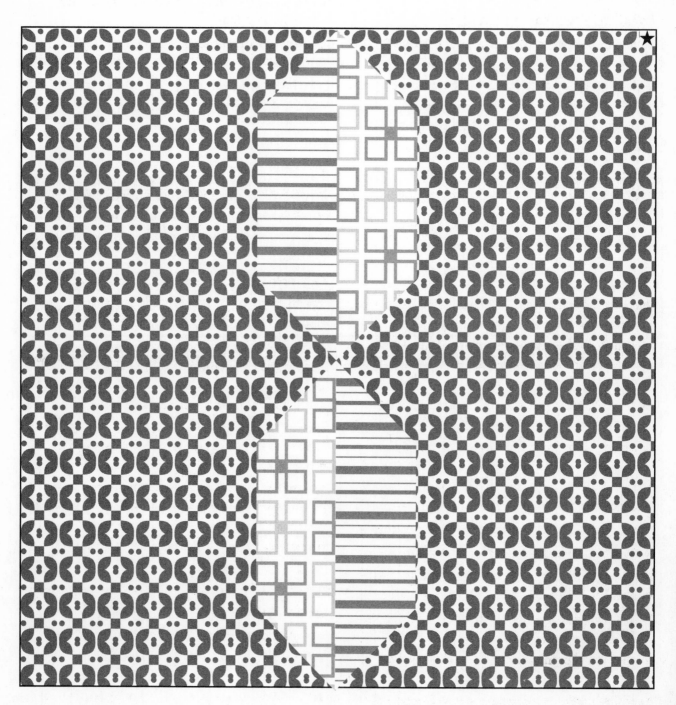

Glossary of Math Terms

acute angle   an angle that is less than 90°

angle   the space formed by two lines stemming from a common point

apex   the top point of a triangle

area   the measurement of a space formed by edges

asymmetry   a condition in which two sides are not equal

base   the bottom edge of a shape

bisect   to divide in half

circle   a round shape measuring 360°

congruent   having the same measurement

cube   a six-sided solid figure, made of congruent square sides

degree   unit of measure for an angle (One degree is equal to 1/360 of a circle.)

diagonal   a slanted line that joins two opposite corners

diamond   a square positioned so that one corner is at the top (A diamond is not a distinct geometric shape.)

equilateral triangle   a triangle with three congruent sides and three congruent angles

fraction   a number that is not a whole number, such as 1/2, formed by dividing one quantity into multiple parts

hexagon   a shape with six sides

horizontal   running across, or left-to-right

intersection   the point where two lines cross

isosceles triangle   a triangle with two congruent sides and two congruent angles

line of symmetry   a line that divides two alike halves

midpoint   a point that lies halfway along a line

negative space   the space created outside a shape

obtuse angle   an angle that is greater than 90°

octagon   a shape with eight sides

oval   an egg-shaped figure with a smooth, continuous edge

parallel   two lines that are always the same distance apart, and therefore never intersect

parallelogram   a quadrilateral that has two pairs of parallel sides and two pairs of congruent sides

pentagon   a shape with five sides

perimeter   the outside edge of a shape

perpendicular   at right angles to a line

quadrilateral   any four-sided figure

ratio   a relationship between two different numbers

rectangle   a quadrilateral that has four right angles (All rectangles are parallelograms.)

right angle   an angle of 90°, which forms a square corner

right triangle   a triangle with a right angle (90°)

scalene triangle   a triangle with no congruent sides and no congruent angles

square   a quadrilateral that has four right angles and four congruent sides (All squares are rectangles.)

symmetry   a balanced arrangement of parts on either side of a central dividing line or around a central point

trapezoid   a quadrilateral with one pair of parallel sides

triangle   a figure with three sides

vertical   running from or top to bottom

volume   the space contained within a three-dimensional object

Square Origami Template

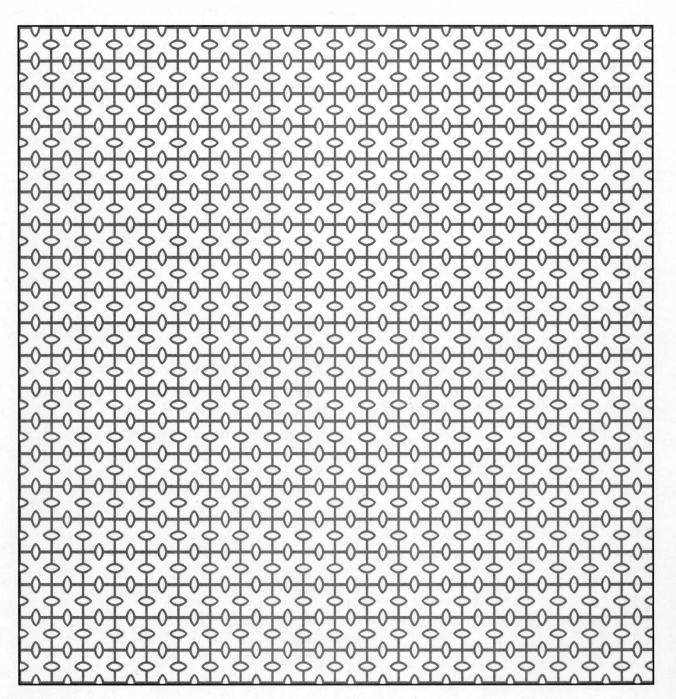